The Circus Is in
A Counting Book

By David L. Harrison
Illustrated by Larry Ross

GOLDEN PRESS • NEW YORK

Western Publishing Company, Inc.
Racine, Wisconsin

ONE gay clown in a funny suit,
With a purple hat, a yellow boot,
A drum to bang, a horn to toot.
The circus is in town!

TWO fine ladies wearing tights,
Swinging high above the lights.
What a way to see the sights,
    Swinging up and down!

THREE striped tigers fast asleep.
Shhh! We mustn't make a peep.
Mustn't make them wake and leap,
        And mustn't *ever* free one!

FOUR fat bears in baggy pants.
They sort of shuffle, sort of dance,
Sort of box, and sort of prance.
I like that little wee one.

FIVE gray elephants in a row,
Gently swaying to and fro,
Holding tails and moving slow.
I'd hate to try to stop one.

SIX sleek jugglers juggling fans,
Paper plates and silver cans,
Balls and cups and frying pans!
They never seem to drop one.

SEVEN ponies in a trot.
Some are good, and some are not.
Some are out of step a lot.
I wish that I could try one.

EIGHT smart dogs in silly clothes,
With ruffled skirts and satin bows,
Walking on their tippy-toes.

      I wish that I could buy one.

NINE slim tumblers on the mat.
None of them are very fat,
Because they'd squash each other flat,
    And that just might upset one!

TEN tall camels looking lumpy.
All their backs are kind of humpy.
Riding them would be quite bumpy!
Still, I'd like to have one.

Now that I can count to ten,
It's fun to start at one again:

ONE gay clown dressed up in style.

TWO fine ladies swing and smile.

THREE striped tigers fast asleep.

FOUR fat bears that prance and leap.

FIVE gray elephants in a row.

SIX sleek jugglers steal the show.

SEVEN ponies in a trot.

EIGHT smart dogs that dance a lot.

NINE slim tumblers very jumpy,

And TEN tall camels looking bumpy!